CHILDN

W9-AEC-393

DATE DUE
7 11 92
DATE DUE
6 14 94
DATE DUE
8 31 93
DATE DUE
4 12 95

PEDRO & THE PADRE

A Tale from Jalisco, Mexico

BY Verna Aardema PICTURES BY Friso Henstra

Dial Books for Young Readers NEW YORK

Published by Dial Books for Young Readers,
A Division of Penguin Books USA Inc.
375 Hudson Street
New York, New York 10014

Designed by Jane Byers Bierhorst
Printed in Hong Kong by South China
Printing Company (1988) Limited
E
First Edition
1 3 5 7 9 10 8 6 4 2

Library of Congress Cataloging in Publication Data

Aardema, Verna.
Pedro & the padre.

Summary / In this Mexican folktale a lazy
boy learns a lesson about lying.
[1. Folklore—Mexico.
2. Honesty—Folklore.]
I. Title.
PZ8.1.A213Pe 1991 398.2'0972 [E] 87-24476
ISBN 0-8037-0522-0 / ISBN 0-8037-0523-9 (lib. bdg.)

The art for each picture consists of an
ink and watercolor painting, which is
color-separated and reproduced in full color.

For Sylvia
F. H.

Para mi nieta, Jill Aardema,
que estudió Español en la escuela.
V. A.

GLOSSARY

arré (ar-RAY): giddyap
gracias (GRAH-seeahs): thanks
Jalisco (Hah-LEES-co): a state in Mexico
padre (PAH-dray): priest
Pedro (PAY-dro): boy's name
pícaro (PEE-car-o): mischievous person
sí (SEE): yes
sombrero (som-BRER-o): a hat with a very wide brim
Uf! (oof): Ugh!
pillo (PEE-yo): rogue, rascal, or petty thief

"Pedro, you don't earn the beans you eat!" scolded his father. "Every time I look at you, you are leaning on your hoe!" The two were hoeing the bean patch. And as usual, Pedro was not doing even a boy's share of the work.

Pedro's father continued, "I'm giving up on you, Pedro. You are going to have to go to work for someone else. Maybe for a stranger you will learn to work."

And the next morning Pedro was sent forth with the hope that somehow he would find a job. All day he walked a dusty road. At sunset he came to a village. A priest was coming out of a little church. Pedro went to him and said, "Padre, do you know where I can find lodging?"

The priest looked at Pedro. He saw a youth sturdily built, with black eyes shining in a mischievous face. He said, "Young man, are you running away?"

"No, Padre," said Pedro. "I am Pedro de Urdemalas. I'm the son of a farmer. But I'm like a coyote pup pushed out of the den. My father said I must find work."

"There's plenty of work you could do around here," said the padre. "I cannot pay you. But you may eat at my table and sleep in my house."

"*Gracias,*" said Pedro. "I will do anything you ask me to do."

He followed the padre to his house beside the church. And he was genuinely happy to have found a job.

For many days Pedro lived with the padre, working in the church and garden. His favorite duty was ringing the church bell. He would ring the getting-up bell first. Then, after the villagers had had time to get ready, he would ring the come-to-church bell.

Pedro loved to pull the bell rope and let it carry his hands back up: BONG—BONG, BONG—BONG! But if he pulled the rope too hard, the bell would go, BONG—*klunk*. Then he would know that it had tipped over. And he would have to climb the ladder to the belfry and set it right again.

There were bats in the belfry. Pedro was afraid of them. Also, the people of the village teased him when he silenced the bell. They knew that the padre had never done that.

One Sunday morning, when the priest woke Pedro to have him ring the first bell, he made the mistake of closing his eyes again. The next thing he knew, the padre was calling him to ring the last bell. Pedro rang the bell.

When no one came to the service, the padre said, "Pedro, you rang the first bell, didn't you?"

"*Sí, sí!*" said Pedro. "But I guess nobody got up."

Two women walked by on their way to the well. Then the padre said, "You didn't ring the bell! You lied to me!"

"I'm sorry," said Pedro. "I won't ever tell a lie again."

Another day the padre rode off on his burro, Panchita, to call on the sick people of his parish. He left Pedro hoeing the corn patch.

But the sun was hot. And scarcely was the padre out of sight, when Pedro went into a storeroom and lay down on a sack of beans. Although it was not siesta time, he was soon asleep.

When the priest returned, he found Pedro sleeping. He shook him and said, "Why didn't you finish the hoeing?"

"I did finish," said Pedro. "The weeds must have grown up again. They grow fast on hot days."

"Pedro, Pedro!" cried the padre. "That is a monstrous lie! Where did you learn how to lie?"

"From a book," said Pedro.

"You learned to tell lies from a book?" cried the padre.

"*Sí*," said Pedro. "HOW TO TELL LIES is on the cover! If you will lend me your burro, I will fetch it for you."

"Take Panchita and go get the book," said the padre.

Pedro mounted the burro. And holding the reins very tightly, he cried, "*Arré! Arré!*" But with the reins so tight, the animal would not budge.

Pedro went to the padre and said, "Panchita won't go. Perhaps if you lend me your hat, she will think I am you."

The priest gave Pedro his broad-brimmed black hat. Pedro put it on, mounted the burro, and rode off.

After they had gone a little way, Pedro said, "Panchita, would you believe there's such a thing as a lie book?"

Panchita put one ear forward and said, *eee-aaaah!*

At siesta time they came to an abandoned hut. There was a thorny, leafless tree beside it, and an old well in the backyard. Pedro tied Panchita to the tree and gave her water from a rusty bucket that was lying near the well.

Then Pedro went into the hut and lay down on the dirt floor for a nap. Presently he was wakened by the sound of wagon wheels. *Gunko, gunko, gunko.* The wagon stopped!

Pedro sat up. Someone was coming! He heard the *gwuf, gwuf, gwuf* of footsteps in the sand.

A man appeared in the doorway. He was as stocky as a barrel cactus and he wore the faded garb of a farmer.

Pedro relaxed. And immediately he looked about for something to sell to the stranger.

When the man asked, "Do you live in this shack?"

Pedro replied, "No. But I own it. I just come by now and then to water my money tree."

"Money tree!" exclaimed the man. "What money tree?"

"My burro is tied to it," said Pedro. Then he went out to the well, filled the bucket, and watered the tree.

The man watched skeptically. "I don't see anything on that tree but thorns," he said.

"Thorns!" cried Pedro. "Look again! Those are real live money buds. I shall be rich."

The man looked more closely. "Will you sell that tree?" he asked. "I could take it home in my wagon."

"Well," said Pedro, "the truth is, I need money now. Give me one hundred pesos, and the tree is yours."

The man paid Pedro and began digging up the tree.

Pedro rode off as fast as Panchita would trot. He said, "Panchita, would you believe that money grows on trees?"

Panchita put one ear forward. She said, *eee-aaaah!*

Pedro traveled about, living on that money for a time. But one day, when the money was gone, he saw a small donkey caravan approaching down the road. Immediately he looked about for something to sell to the traders.

A large toad happened to be sunning itself on the ground near-by. Pedro popped the padre's hat over it. Then he sat down beside it and began peeling his last orange.

When the traders reached Pedro, they stopped to visit. While they talked, Pedro kept eating his orange and slipping bits of it under the hat.

One of the men asked, "Why are you feeding your hat?"

"My magic bird is under there," said Pedro.

"Magic bird! Magic bird!" cried both men together.

"*Sí,*" said Pedro. "She talks, she sings, she dances!"

"Let us see her," said one of the men.

"No," said Pedro. "She might fly away."

"Will you sell her?" asked the other man.

"It would break my heart," said Pedro. "But I need money now. Give me one hundred pesos, and the bird is yours."

The man paid Pedro and the other man reached for the hat.

"Wait!" cried Pedro. "Don't let her out until I am long gone. Or she will follow me."

Pedro rode off as fast as Panchita would trot. He said, "Panchita, would you believe there is such a thing as a magic bird?"

Panchita put one ear forward. She said, *eee-aaaah!*

However, before Pedro was out of sight, the man who bought the bird put his hand under the hat. His fingers closed over the

skin of the warty toad. "*Uf!*" he shrieked. "Catch that *pillo*!"

His partner cried, "*Arré! Arré!*" And he was off at a gallop. The man jammed the hat on top of his *sombrero* and followed—with the loaded donkeys trailing behind.

The men caught Pedro, took away the money, and stuffed him feet first into an old grain sack. Then, draping him over Panchita's back, they went on.

That evening the caravan camped beside a river. The man who had bought the toad dragged the sack with Pedro in it to the water's edge. He was about to throw it in, when his partner called, "Don't drown him now. Do it in the morning. Let him worry about it all night."

So Pedro was saved temporarily. And worry he did!

He said over and over, "God, if you will get me out of this, I will never tell a lie again."

Pedro lay quietly inside the bag until he heard the traders snoring. Then, like a worm, he hitched closer to where the animals were, and said, "*Hsst,* Panchita."

Panchita tossed her head and snuffled, *huh-huh-huh.*

Pedro wormed his way to her side. Then he poked a corner of the bag close to her mouth. The sack was saturated with grain dust.

Panchita smelled corn. She said, *eee-aaaah!*

Pedro cringed. But the men snored on.

Panchita bit into the burlap and chewed, *ngilen, ngilen, ngilen.*

Soon there was a hole big enough for Pedro to get his hands through. He reached out and untied the rope that bound the mouth of the bag. He was free!

Quietly Pedro retrieved the padre's hat. Then he loosened Panchita, and he and the burro set out for home.

They traveled all night. At dawn they saw their own village in the distance. Panchita forgot that she was tired and broke into a brisk trot. As they approached the padre's house, he came out of the door.

Panchita trotted to him, braying happily, *eee-aaaah, eee-aaaah!*

She nuzzled her muzzle into the padre's outstretched hand.

The padre said, "So, Panchita, you have brought the *pícaro* home!"

Pedro answered, "*Sí.* And Padre, I am looking for a book that says on the cover, HOW TO TELL THE TRUTH."

The padre saw penitence in Pedro's face. "Good," he said. "And now it is time to ring the getting-up bell."

"I will do it," said Pedro. He slipped off Panchita's back and hurried to the church.

Pedro clasped the bell rope with both hands and pulled hard. The bell went, BONG—*klunk*.

Then the people of the village and the bats in the belfry knew that Pedro had come home.